A Tin Home

Book Three
Revised Edition

Christian Liberty Press
Arlington Heights, Illinois 60004

A publication of
Christian Liberty Press
502 West Euclid Avenue
Arlington Heights, Illinois 60004
www.christianlibertypress.com

A TIME AT HOME
    1. Phonics–Juvenile literature
    2. Reading–Juvenile literature
Written by
    Florence M. Lindstrom
Copyediting by
    Belit M. Shewan
    Edward J. Shewan

Cover Design by
    Eric D. Bristley
Illustrations by
    Vic Lockman
Colorization of Illustrations by
    Christopher D. Kou
Graphics and layout by
    Eric D. Bristley
    Christopher D. Kou
    Edward J. Shewan

ISBN 1-930092-29-6

Printed in the United States of America

Contents

Lesson 1

A a

game

Practice sounding these words, listening for the long vowel sound. Say them until you know them.

gāmȩ	nō	prāy
came	go	play
name	so	may
James	yo–yo	day
same		way
tame		say
lame		Ray

A game is fun with a pal.
James is a pal to Sam.
James and Sam will play.
Wag will play, too.
No, Wag, let James have it.

A Game With James

A pal came to see Sam.
His name is James.
Sam is glad James came to play.

Sam and James will play a game.
Sam will hit the ball to James,
but Wag ran in the way!

"No, Wag, let James have it!
James must have it to play!"
Sam is not mad at Wag.

It is fun if Wag plays games, too.

1

Lesson 2

A a

game

Practice sounding these words, listening for the long vowel sound. Say them until you know them.

gāte	hē	rāke
ate	see	take
late	we	bake
Kate	be	make
wait		lake
bait	time	cake
	home	
pīe		blessing

We take time to pray and play.
We pray and play at home.
Ray has bait to get a fish.
God gives us lots of blessings.

Time to Go Home

Can you see Ray and Kate?
Ray and Kate will go home.
It is late as they go to the gate.

Ray and Kate came from the lake.
Ray has bait in his box.
Did he get a fish? No, he did not.

Mother and Father wait for them.
Ray will not have fish to give.

At home we can help.
It is time to help Mother.
Mother and Father work for us.
We must make time to work, too.

Kate helps Mother bake a pie.
Ray will help Father rake.
Ray and Kate make Mother and Father
glad.

Mother tells us it is time to sit.
Father will pray and thank God.
He will ask God to bless them.
God gives them lots of blessings.

At home we can work and play.
If we work, Mother will say we may
play.
A time to work and a time to play.
It is fun this way.

A a

game

Practice sounding these words, listening for the long vowel sound. Say them until you know them.

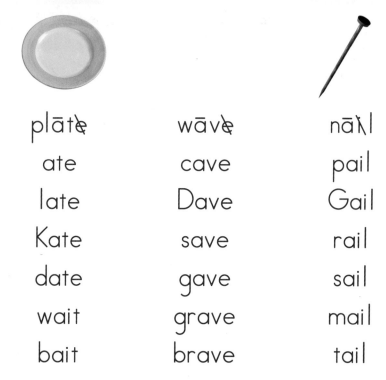

plāte	wāve	nāil
ate	cave	pail
late	Dave	Gail
Kate	save	rail
date	gave	sail
wait	gave	mail
bait	grave	tail

Dave can taste his lunch.
Mother gave him a big plate.
God gave Dave his gift of taste.
Dave is glad that he can taste.
We thank God that we can taste.

God Made Us to Taste

Thank you for the lunch you made.
The lunch makes the plate hot.
Gail will be glad to taste the lunch.
May we have cake, too, Mother?

You may have cake, Dave.
But you must not have a lot of cake.

Mother gave Dave and Gail hot lunch.
The taste makes them glad.

God made you to taste, Dave.
He made you taste as you ate.
We must thank God for this gift.

Lesson 4

A a

game

Practice sounding these words, listening for the long vowel sound. Say them until you know them.

pā\nt	rā\n	flāk\e
saint	gain	sake
faint	main	take
	pain	wake
	stain	rake
important	train	quake

It may rain today.
Rain and flakes make the land wet.
God sends the rain to bless us.
James will help his dad.
They will not paint in the rain.

8

Dad Must Wait

Will you paint today, Dad?
Will you fix and paint the gate?

I will not paint today, James.
It will rain and get the paint wet.

Will you be sad for the rain, Dad?
Will the rain make you mad?

I will not be sad for the rain.
We must have rain for the sake of the
plants. The rain is so important.
God sends the rain for his land.

Lesson 5

E e

beans

Practice sounding these words, listening for the long vowel sound. Say them until you know them.

bēe	ēar	shēep
trees	dear	deep
breeze	hear	sleep
	fear	
sea	near	bleat
tea	clear	treat
flea	tear	tweet

Did you hear the sheep?
Is it clear for you to hear?
It is a treat to hear the sheep bleat.
Steve hears a "tweet" in a tree.
Ears are a gift from God.

Can You Hear?

Can you hear that, Grandpa?
Do you hear "tweet, tweet" ?

I do not hear it, Steve.
It is not clear to my ears.
My ears do not hear so well.
I must get near to hear it.

Thank God that your ears do hear.
You can still hear the bees and the
breeze in the trees.
It is a treat to hear the sheep bleat.
Ears are a gift from God.
Make your ears hear good things.

Lesson 6

E e

beans

Practice sounding these words, listening for the long vowel sound. Say them until you know them.

bēan	sēed	tāil
clean	need	trail
mean	weed	pail
lean	deed	Gail
Jean	feed	
		rain
away		stain

Is Wag glad to get clean?
He will not stay.
He will run away.
Mud will make a stain.
Sam must clean the stain.

Sam Cleans Wag

Stay, Wag, stay.
You must not run away.
Wait for me to clean you.
The suds will help to clean you.

No, Wag, you must not go in.
You must not make the home wet.

I can see Wag, Sam.
He has made a mud trail.
Mother will not be glad.
We must help Mother clean.
We need a pail to clean the stain.

Lesson 7

E e  beans

Practice sounding these words, listening for the long vowel sound. Say them until you know them.

mēat	bēans	mēal
eat	Jean	Neal
heat	green	heal
treat		seal
greet	speak	real
meet	weak	deal

Mother will need help.
Jean will speak to Dave.
He can hear Jean and will help.
It is a treat to greet Father.
Father is dear to us.

Time to Work

Come, Jean and Dave.
I need to speak to you.
Will you help me make the meal?

We will help you, Mother.
Dave can help me bake a cake.
We must set the heat to bake.
The meat and cake must bake.
We will clean the green beans.
Come, Dave, we must work fast.

At six we will hear Father come.
It is a treat to run and greet him.

Lesson 8

E e  beans

Practice sounding these words, listening for the long vowel sound. Say them until you know them.

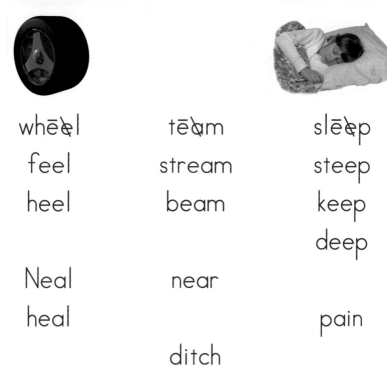

wheel	team	sleep
feel	stream	steep
heel	beam	keep
		deep
Neal	near	
heal		pain
	ditch	

Neal can feel the cut on his heel.
God will heal his cut.
We can feel heat and steam.
God made us to feel.
It is a gift we need to help us.

The Gift to Feel

Neal will rest near a stream.
He can feel the heat of the sun.
He can feel the green grass.
He will feel the wet stream.
He is glad God helps him feel.

Neal has a deep cut on his heel.
He fell in a steep ditch.
Neal can feel the cut.
God will heal his cut.

God helps us to feel pain.
The pain tells us we need help.

Lesson 9

E e

beans

Practice sounding these words, listening for the long vowel sound. Say them until you know them.

fēet	pēas	weēk
beets	sea	peek
meet	tea	seek
greet	flea	meek

Peter   stake   crē āte

place (s)

Peter has seeds to plant.
He will dig deep in the sod.
He plants beets, peas, and beans.
He needs to wait a week.
He will see the plants then.

Peter Plants Seeds

Peter needs to plant his seeds.

He will plant beets, peas, and green beans.

He had to dig deep in the sod to get up the weeds.

The sod must be clear of weeds.

Peter has made a stake near the seeds. The stake has the name of the seeds.

The next day came.
Peter went to see the seeds.
He did not see the beets and peas.
He did not see the beans.
He went to tell his father.

No, Peter, not yet.
You will not see the plants yet.
You will see them next week.
You must take up the weeds and keep
the plants wet.

At last Peter can see the plants.
The plants got big.
He will not eat the beets, peas, and
beans yet.
He will keep them wet, and the sun will
help make them get big.

Did God create the seeds?
Yes, God did create seeds.
He makes them get big.
God is wonderful.

Lesson 10

I i

bike

Practice sounding these words, listening for the long vowel sound. Say them until you know them.

fly	bike	smile
try	Mike	mile
my	hike	pile
why	like	tile
cry	pike	while
sky	dike	awhile

I will try to hike a mile.
Peter will like a bike hike.
It takes time to go up to Pikes Peak.
Peter likes to see the sky and big peak
that God made.

The Bike Hike

Let us go on a bike hike, Dad.
May we try to go for ten miles?
My red bike can go fast.

Ten miles will take awhile, Peter.
We will take a lunch and drink.
Mother will take us in the van.
It will be a hike you will like.

Peter and his dad went in the van.
Mother went up Pikes Peak.
Dad and Peter got on the bikes.
Peter had the best bike hike.

Lesson 11

I i  bike

Practice sounding these words, listening for the long vowel sound. Say them until you know them.

five	ride	mine
hive	hide	nine
alive	side	fine
	wide	dine
find	slide	
wind	vine	
time	pine	

Mike will try to find Gail.
She likes to hide.
She can hide from Mike.
She cannot hide from God.
God can see us.

24

Hide and Seek

Can you find me, Mike?
You do not see me as I hide.

Mike has a smile as he hears Gail.
She is five and likes to hide.
He will clean his bike.
Then he will try to find Gail.

This time she is by the pine tree.
He tags Gail and tells her to sit by his side.

You can hide so I will not see you, but you cannot hide from God.

Lesson 12

I i

bike

Practice sounding these words, listening for the long vowel sound. Say them until you know them.

mīce (s)	kīnd	cry (ī)
nice	bind	try
rice	mind	my
price	find	why
slice	wind	by
dice	blind	dry
spice	grind	fly

Miss Tile is kind to Mike.
Mike is nice to Miss Tile.
Do you like to eat a slice of pie?
Mike is glad to eat the slice.
We will try to be kind and nice.

Mike is Kind

May I cut your grass, Miss Tile?
I will be glad to cut and rake it.

Yes, Mike, I need to have it cut.
I will like it if you will do it.
That is kind of you.

He likes to be nice to her.
Miss Tile is not well.
He likes to try to make her smile.
She is kind to Mike.
Mike got the grass cut.
Miss Tile gave him a slice of pie.

Lesson 13

I i  bike

Practice sounding these words, listening for the long vowel sound. Say them until you know them.

tīre	dīme	kīte
fire	time	bite
wire	lime	site
hire	chime	white

glasses  eyes

The white kite has a fire on it.
The breeze makes it fly.
With glasses, Pam can see it fly.
She is glad God gave her eyes.
We must see nice things.

A Fire on a Kite

Sam has a big white kite.
Pam will help Jan paint Sam's kite.
They will paint a red fire on it.

Sam got it up in the sky.
See the breeze make it fly.
Pam needs glasses to see it.
When the kite is in the sky, the fire is like a red dot.

God gave us eyes to see.
We must thank Him for eyes.
We must see nice things with them.

Lesson 14

I i  bike

Practice sounding these words, listening for the long vowel sound. Say them until you know them.

līght	chīld	grīnd
night	mild	mind
might	wild	wind
fight		find
right	high	blind

A kind child will try to do right.
It is not nice to fight.
God gave us a wonderful mind.
We must do right things with it.
Nate has his mother as a teacher.

At Home With Nate

Do you see the child on the seat?
If Nate has time he likes to read.
He sits near a light that is bright.
He is so glad that he is not blind.
Nate will try to do what is right.

His mother is his teacher.
Each day Nate sits at his desk.
He will find his work and do it.
God gave him a mind to be kind.

Nate may be a fireman one day.
He will help to fight fires.

Lesson 15

O o

rope

Practice sounding these words, listening for the long vowel sound. Say them until you know them.

gōat	rōpe	bōw
coat	hope	row
boat		tow
float	pole	throw
moat	hole	low

tie   tied

Row, row the boat.
Dan will lift the rope and get in.
The pals hope to ride a mile.
Nate gave the rope to Dan.
Did Dan get wet?

The Boat Ride

Dave and Nate got in a row boat.
A rope keeps the boat by a pole.
Dan will lift the rope.
He will jump in the boat, too.
It is fun to have a boat ride.

The pals hope to row and row.
The tan boat may go miles and miles.
They will sit still in the boat.

Will Dan miss the boat?
Dan did not get to the boat.
He fell in and got wet.

Dave will give Dan a rope.
He will throw the rope to Dan.
The rope will help Dan.
The end of the rope is tied to the
boat.
Dave and Nate must lift Dan.

At last, Dan got in the boat.
It is time to row the boat.
They will row it to the dock.

Dan needs to go home.
Nate and Dave will take him.
Nate gave Dan his coat.
It will help Dan get dry.

The pals had a day of fun.

Lesson 16

O o

rope

Practice sounding these words, listening for the long vowel sound. Say them until you know them.

hōle	nose	
pole	hose	toe
mole	pose	Joe
stole		hoe
	grow	
oak	tōad	
Rōse	road	

Can you see the hole?
Joe and Rose can see a toad.
Will a toad eat a rose?
A toad will grow if it eats bugs.
The oak tree is next to the road.

A Toad on the Road

Come and see this, Rose.
Look at the toad next to the road.
We must get the toad to hop.
It must hop away from the road.

Will the toad hop in a box?
Can we keep it as a pet, Rose?
We can take it home and feed it.

No, Joe, it is best that it is free.
It must eat bugs to grow.
See it hop to the oak tree.
It will hop in the hole by the tree.

Lesson 17

O o  rope

Practice sounding these words, listening for the long vowel sound. Say them until you know them.

smōke	cōld	tōast
spoke	told	boast
woke	old	roast
joke	fold	coast
	sold	

checkers

Did you eat toast and eggs?
Do you like to play checkers?
Do you try to win as you play?
Dad spoke to Dan.
He told Dan not to boast.

Do Not Boast

Dan and Jan woke up at nine.
They had toast, milk, and eggs.
The rain made them stay inside.
They play the game of checkers.

Dan spoke to Jan that he will win.
Jan will try to win, too.
Dan did win in six games.
He told Dad that he did the best.

Dad told Dan not to boast.
God is not glad if we boast.

Lesson 18

O o  rope

Practice sounding these words, listening for the long vowel sound. Say them until you know them.

hōse	stōnes	mōw
nose		low
pose	soap	grow
rose		slow
	soak	
right		pail

Dad will mow the grass.
Joe will clean the van.
He has soap, a hose, and a pail.
He got Dad wet.
He did not clean the van right.

Joe Helps Dad

Joe can see Dad mow the grass.
Dad must pick up stones and sticks.
He must work and work.

Joe will work too.
He will clean the van.
He got a pail and the soap.
The hose will help him work.

Stop, Joe, keep the hose low!
You try to help, but it is not right.
You soak the van and Dad, too.

Lesson 19

O o  rope

Practice sounding these words, listening for the long vowel sound. Say them until you know them.

tōạst	nōsẹ	smōkẹ
roast	rose	joke
boast	hose	poke
	close	woke
stove		yoke
	delicious	

Smell the delicious toast and roast!
Can you smell smoke and a rose?
God gave us the gift of smell.
The nose helps us to smell.
It is important to have this gift.

The Gift to Smell

Dan came into his home.
He can smell a roast on the stove.
It smells delicious to his nose.

He can smell the rose in the vase.
He can smell smoke from the fire.
He is glad he has a nose to smell.

Dan has black spots on his hands.
The spots do not smell nice.
He will clean the spots.
The nose is a gift from God.

Lesson 20

U u

 tube

Practice sounding these words, listening for the long vowel sound. Say them until you know them.

tūne   mūle   frūıt

June   rule   suit

prune   juice

            use

            fuse

Luke has a tan mule to ride.
Sam made NoNo go with fruit.
We need to keep pets clean.
We need to feed the pets.
Luke and Sam like to ride NoNo.

Fun With a Mule

In June Sam went to see Luke.
Luke has a tan mule to ride.
The name of the mule is NoNo.

Luke let Sam ride NoNo.
NoNo did not go the right way.
Luke told Sam that NoNo likes fruit.
Sam made NoNo go with the fruit.

Sam and Luke had fun with NoNo.
Luke gave it feed to eat.
He keeps it clean and safe.

Lesson 21

U u

tube

Practice sounding these words, listening for the long vowel sound. Say them until you know them.

flūte	tūne	pew (ū)
cute	prune	new
mute	June	few
	dune	dew
music		flew

Dan and Jan can play a new tune.

Wag is glad to hear the music.

Wag is cute as he sings a tune.

We will hear nice music.

Do you like to hear nice music?

The Gift of Music

Father and Mother like music.
Dan and Jan like music, too.
Dan can play a gray flute.
Jan can play a tune, too.

Dan can play a new tune.
Jan will play with him.
Wag sings as Dan and Jan play.
Wag is cute as he sings his tune.

It is fun to hear music.
God is glad if we hear nice tunes.

Lesson 22

U u

tube

Practice sounding these words, listening for the long vowel sound. Say them until you know them.

sūᵢt	glūe	blew (ū)
fruit	blue	flew
juice	true	new
	clue	threw

| meeting | lie | whąt (ŭ) |

Father needs a new blue suit.
We must say what is true.
We must not tell a lie.
God is not glad if we tell a lie.
We must be sad, too.

A New Suit

Father has to have a new blue suit.
He has to speak at a meeting.
Mother and Father went to shop.

Miss June came to stay.
She will play with Mike and Gail.
Gail told Miss June a tale.
She said Father will get a new van.

That is not true, Gail, said Mike.
We must say what is true.
Father will get a new suit.
You must be sad if you tell a lie.

Lesson 23

U u  tube

Practice sounding these words, listening for the long
vowel sound. Say them until you know them.

mūle   glūe   Bī ble

rule   true

         blue

         delicious

The Bible is true.

We can read God's rules.

The rules will help us to obey.

Mother made a delicious meal.

God gave us life. We praise Him.

A Time at Home

The meal smells delicious, Mother.
Thank you for what you made.
Let us pray to thank God for it.

Let us go and sit in here.
It is time to read the Bible.
What the Bible says is true.
It tells us of God's rules.
The Bible tells us to obey God.

God will help us not to sin.
We praise God for His Bible.

Lesson 24

U u  tube

Practice sounding these words, listening for the long vowel sound. Say them until you know them.

flūte	blūe	flew (ū)
cute	glue	drew
	Sue	grew
use	true	new
	clue	

snowman

It is fun to use glue.
We can use a pen and pad, too.
Sue drew on the pad.
Sue made a cute gift with puffs.
It is for dear Grandma.

Gift for Grandma

Do you see the new tan box?
It had a pen, glue, and pad in it.
Sue will use the pen and pad.

She drew a snowman on the pad.
Sue cut the snowman.
Sue will glue puffs on it.
It will be a gift for Grandma.

Grandma gives Sue a big hug.
She tells Sue the gift is cute.
Grandma will have it on her desk.
Grandma and Sue are dear pals.

U u  tube

Practice sounding these words, listening for the long vowel sound. Say them until you know them.

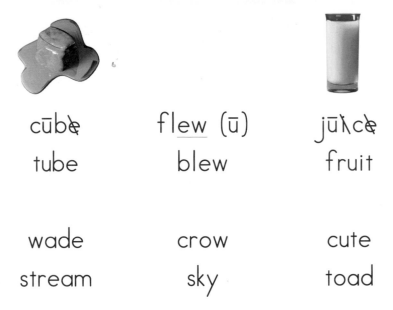

| cūbe | flew (ū) | jūice |
| tube | blew | fruit |

| wade | crow | cute |
| stream | sky | toad |

It feels nice to wade in a stream.
We like cold cubes in juice.
Sue can see a crow and a toad.
Rose sees a few ants on a stone.
Sue and Rose like to be pals.

A Hot Day

This June day is hot and dry.
The wind blew, but it felt hot.
Sue and Rose sat near a tree.

A crow flew up to the sky.
A cute toad sat near a stream.
A few ants went up on a stone.

Sue's mother gave them juice with cubes.
They thank her, for they are not rude.
Rose will now wade in the stream.
This will help her to feel nice.

Lesson 26

Practice sounding these words, listening for the long vowel sound. Say them until you know them.

fall   winter   spring

summer

The days pass quickly.
The birds make nests in the spring.
The leaves drop in the fall.
We make a snowman in the winter.
Summer, winter, spring and fall,
I like them best of all.

What I Like Best

The leaves float in the breeze
As they drop from the trees.
We read and play and take tests.
I like fall the best.

Snow makes the land look clean.
The pine trees still stay so green.
We work and play and rest.
I like winter the best.

God makes the buds to grow
And the sweet breezes to blow.
I plant seeds as birds make a nest.
I like spring the best.

The hot sun and green grass
Help make each day quickly pass.
We work and swim and rest.
I like summer the best.

Lesson 27

Practice sounding these words, listening for the long vowel sound. Say them until you know them.

sound   vowels   long

family

A long vowel sound says its name.
Every vowel can say a sound.
You can read to your family.
They will be glad that you read.
You can read lots of words.
It is best that you keep working.
You will have lots of fun.

Long Vowel Sounds

Tail, train, cake, and play
Have the long vowel sound of a.

Flea, meat, sleep, and tree
Have the long vowel sound of e.

Dime, kite, bride, and fly
Have the long vowel sound of i.

Goat, nose, stove, and snow
Have the long vowel sound of o.

Fruit, mule, blew, and glue
Have the long vowel sound of u.

You can read, that we can say.
Thank God for your mind each day.